EMMI THE PINK ELEPHANT

-Book One-

Written and Illustrated by
Barbara Klein

Printed in the United States of America

ISBN-13: 978-1537146904
ISBN-1537146904

10 9 8 7 6 5 4 3 2

Empire Publishing

www.empirebookpublishing.com

All Scripture passages are the author's own paraphrase.

CHAPTERS

EMMI'S FIRST CHRISTMAS

There was once in the jungle an elephant called Emmi. She had big ears, a long trunk, a short tail, and was very pink.

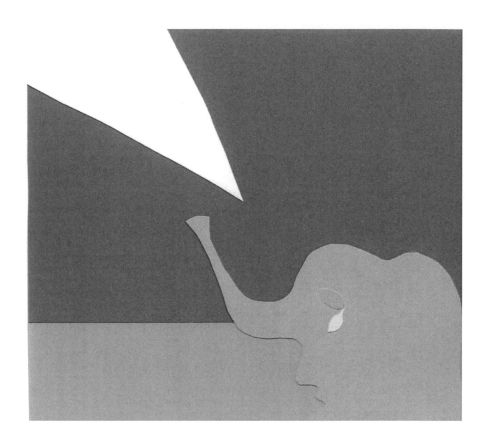

Normally, Emmi was a happy Elephant, but lately she had become sad. She was lonely and became afraid of sounds in the night. She often wanted to cry. One night, when she could not sleep, she saw a bright Light in the sky. It shown down on a place in the middle of the jungle. She decided to follow this Light.

Emmi, the pink Elephant, was not the only one in the jungle who decided to follow the Light. Chester, the Cheetah, did too. He also had become sad because he had broken his leg and could not run fast anymore.

Monty, the Monkey, saw the light as he was swinging through the trees. He too was sad because he had stolen some bananas and he felt bad about it. He also decided to follow the Light.

Paddy, the Parrot, was sitting under a tree with a broken wing when he saw the Light. He could only hop slowly toward it, but he felt that he must get to that Light.

Finally, from different ways, they all
reached the clearing in the jungle upon
which the Light shown down. Their eyes
grew big. There in the center of the
clearing was a manger, and in the
manger, a baby that was all shinning with
Light. Kneeling by the manger were a
lady and a man.

The picture was so beautiful and peaceful. It made them very happy. But "What could it mean?" they wondered.

At that very moment, a great Eagle flew down from the sky. He was carrying a large book.

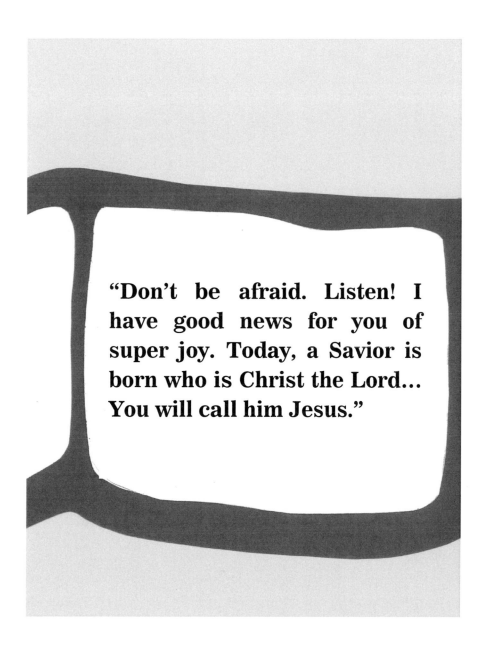

"Don't be afraid. Listen! I have good news for you of super joy. Today, a Savior is born who is Christ the Lord… You will call him Jesus."

In a flash, the picture changed and they did not see anymore a baby in a manger. They saw a man hanging on a cross.

Then the Eagle read in the book. "God loves you so much that He gave His only Son. Anyone who believes in Jesus will not be lost, but will live with God forever."

Then Emmi, the pink Elephant, Chester, the Cheetah, Monty, the Monkey and Paddy, the Parrot, all knelt around the place where they had seen the baby Jesus.

Each of them asked Jesus to come into their hearts.

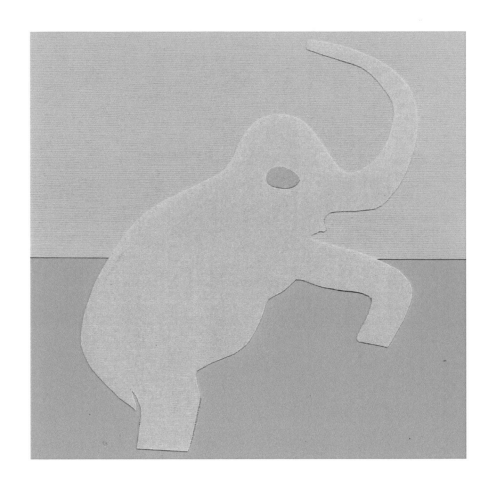

The next moment Emmi, the pink Elephant, was not sad anymore. She was not afraid. She was a big, strong, happy pink Elephant.

Chester, the Cheetah, saw that his leg was healed. He began to run fast in circles all around the clearing.

Monty, the Monkey, began to jump up and down. His heart was so happy. Tomorrow, he will give back the bananas.

Paddy, the Parrot, was flying around them all in great joy.

Emmi, the pink elephant, was not lonely anymore. Now she had friends. They all loved each other because Jesus had come into their hearts. They began to hop, skip, dance, run and fly through the jungle. They all knew that this was the beginning of a new life of adventure for them all.

NOTES TO ADULTS

The Scripture references in this story are found in: Luke 2:10-11; Matthew 1:21; and John 3:16

QUESTIONS YOU MIGHT TALK ABOUT WITH THE CHILDREN

1. Who made Emmi happy, Chester healed, Monty happy and Paddy able to fly?

2. Do you think Emmi, Chester, Monty and Paddy will become good friends? Why?

3. Would you follow the light?

4. What do you wish that Jesus would do for you

5. Would you like to ask Jesus to come into your heart?

EMMI MEETS THE LION

One day, Emmi, the pink Elephant, was going through the jungle with her friends Chester, the Cheetah, Monty, the Monkey, and Paddy the Parrot. They had been playing Tag and Hide & Seek. They were having a great time together.

As they went along, they came to some Leopards. But, the Leopards were not playing in the jungle as Emmi, the pink Elephant and her friends had been doing. They were all huddled down hiding behind trees.

"What's the matter?" asked Chester, the Cheetah. "Larry, the Lion, has told us that he is King of the jungle and nobody can play in the jungle without his permission," said the Leopards. "This does not sound good," said Emmi, the pink Elephant.

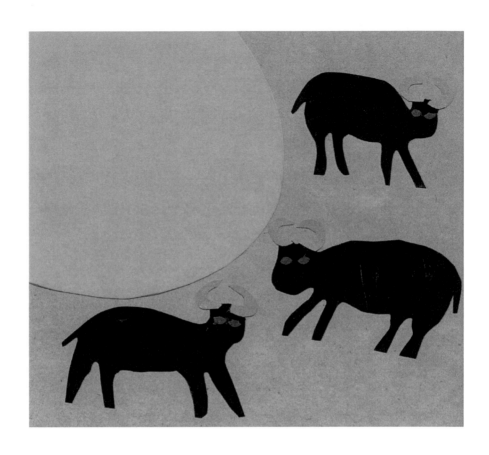

Since it was a very hot day, Emmi, the pink Elephant, and her friends decided to visit the waterhole. When they came to it, they found Water Buffalo there. The Water Buffalo were very thirsty, but they were afraid to go for a drink.

"What's wrong?" asked Monty, the Monkey. "Larry, the Lion, told us he is King of the jungle and nobody can use the waterhole without his permission," said the Water Buffalo. "This is worse than I thought," said Emmi, the pink Elephant.

Emmi, the pink Elephant, and her friends went on and came to some Giraffes. They were under trees that had very fresh, juicy leaves that Giraffes love to eat. But, they were all standing with their long necks down to the ground. "What's the problem?" asked Paddy, the Parrot.

"Larry, the Lion, says he is the King of the jungle and nobody can eat without his permission," answered the Giraffes. "Something must be done about this," said Emmi, the pink Elephant, "I'm going to talk to Larry, the Lion." "But he is the King and he can eat you up!" cried the frightened Giraffes. "I am an Elephant and I am bigger than he is. Besides, he's not the King he thinks he is," said Emmi, the pink Elephant.

So Emmi, the pink Elephant, went off to find Larry, the Lion. When she found him, he was sitting on his throne which was an old stool that had a broken leg, which made his throne wobble. He had a paper crown on his head.

"Are you Larry, the Lion?" asked Emmi, the pink Elephant. "I am Larry, the Lion, the King of the jungle," he said. "I would like to have you meet the real King," said Emmi, the pink Elephant. She began to open a book which had been given to her by a great Eagle and she began to read.

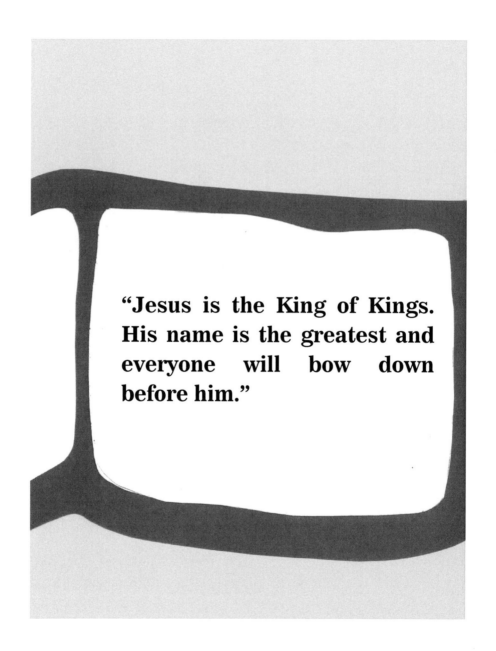

"Jesus is the King of Kings. His name is the greatest and everyone will bow down before him."

"Would you like to meet Jesus?" Emmi, the pink Elephant, asked Larry, the Lion, "He will show you how to be a real and good King." In his heart, Larry, the Lion, knew that he had not been a good King to the jungle animals. He was sorry. So, he knelt down beside Emmi, the pink Elephant, and asked Jesus to come into his heart.

From that moment on, everything changed in the jungle. The Leopards were running all over the place

   The **Water Buffalo** were splashing in
the waterhole.

The Giraffes were enjoying every day
their dinner of fresh, juicy leaves.

Larry, the Lion's name was changed to
"**Sir Lawrence.**" He ruled as a good King
of the jungle from a beautiful throne and
wore a gold crown on his head.

Emmi, the pink Elephant, Chester, the Cheetah, Monty, the monkey and Paddy, the Parrot were happy that Jesus had made everything just as it should be in their jungle.

NOTES TO ADULTS

The Scripture references in this story are found in: Revelation 19:16 and Philippians 2:9-10.

QUESTIONS YOU MIGHT TALK ABOUT WITH THE CHILDREN

1. Why were the leopards, the water buffalo, and the giraffes afraid to play, to drink, and to eat?

2. Why was Emmi not afraid of Larry, the Lion? Would you have been afraid of him?

3. What wrong things happen to you that make you sad?

4. When you are in charge how will you treat others?

5. How did Larry, the Lion become a good king? How would you like Jesus to change you?

More EMMI Books

Part Two

EMMI HELPS A BURRO

EMMI AND HER FRIENDS

EMMI AND RALPH THE RHINO

Made in the USA
Middletown, DE
19 January 2018